I Am a Girl, Hear Me Roar!

by Megan Robin

ROBIN PUBLICATIONS

Library of Congress Control Number: 2017901494

ISBN: 978-0-9983304-3-3 (hardcover)

www.MeganRobin.com

I Am a Girl, Hear Me Roar!

by Megan Robin

I am a girl, hear me roar!
I can move mountains and so much more!

I am unstoppable once I've made up my mind,
but I'm always fair, just, and kind.

I am a force to be reckoned with.
My power is not fiction, fable or myth.

I don't need to be rescued, saved or protected,
because I am strong and connected.

I am connected to women, both powerful and kind,
who raised me, befriended me, and expanded my mind.

I have something sacred inside of me.
Something priceless and beautiful that you cannot see.

It is the thing that lights up my smile.
It drives me forward, mile after mile.

It tells me the difference between right and wrong.
When the going gets tough, it helps me stay strong.

I am a girl, a woman-to-be,
which means I have strength inside of me!

I believe the world is a beautiful place,
because of women's compassion, courage, and grace.

I am surrounded by love and my heart is full.
Positivity and hope nourish my soul.

I am a girl, hear me roar!
Watch me thrive, prosper and soar!

Want more?

Self-Made Lemonade
Let's Start a Business!

by Megan Robin

Hats for Dreamers

By Megan Robin

Visit
www.MeganRobin.com

Hi, I'm Megan Robin!

I write books with positive messages for kids. I believe it is never too soon to start building a life you love.

When I was little, I had an entrepreneurial spirit and did not know where to channel my energy.

For example, in elementary school, I was dragged to the principal's office for using the stickers the teacher gave out for good grades as playground currency.

Early experiences like this one inspired me to write business books and confidence building books for kids.

I believe that lifelong learning is important for both kids and adults.

I graduated from U.C. Santa Barbara with a major in English, received my law degree from U.C. Davis School of Law and obtained my LL.M. in Taxation from Loyola Law School. I am a member of the State Bar of California.

My books share important life and success principles in a fun and engaging way.

You can learn more about me and my books at www.MeganRobin.com.

Visit
www.MeganRobin.com

CPSIA information can be obtained
at www.ICGtesting.com
Printed in the USA
BVOW05*1402310717
490640BV00025B/257/P